A Night at the Beach

Diane Bair and Pamela Wright

D1026796

Contents

Rigby

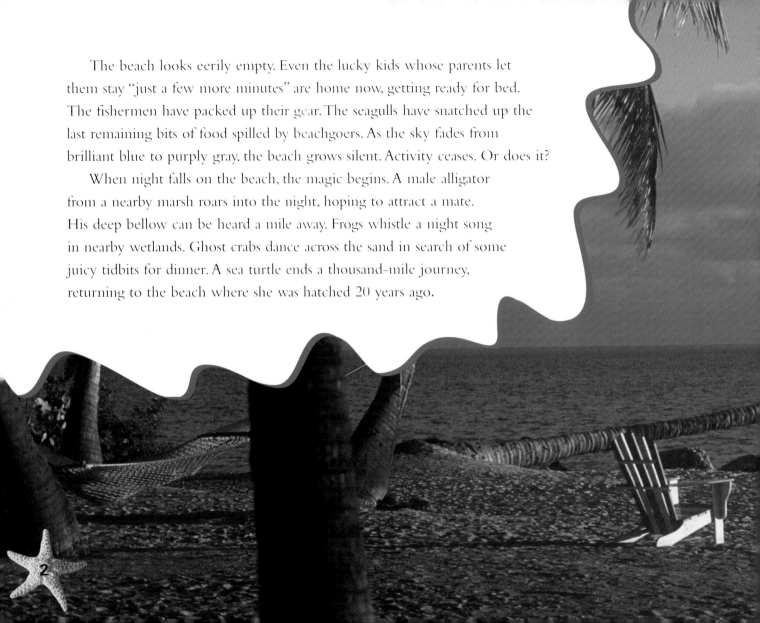

The beach looks eerily empty. Even the lucky kids whose parents let them stay "just a few more minutes" are home now, getting ready for bed. The fishermen have packed up their gear. The seagulls have snatched up the last remaining bits of food spilled by beachgoers. As the sky fades from brilliant blue to purply gray, the beach grows silent. Activity ceases. Or does it?

When night falls on the beach, the magic begins. A male alligator from a nearby marsh roars into the night, hoping to attract a mate. His deep bellow can be heard a mile away. Frogs whistle a night song in nearby wetlands. Ghost crabs dance across the sand in search of some juicy tidbits for dinner. A sea turtle ends a thousand-mile journey, returning to the beach where she was hatched 20 years ago.

Creatures of the Night

At night, some animals seek shelter to sleep and rest. But for others, this is the time to wake up! Creatures that are most active at night are called nocturnal animals.

Most nocturnal animals can find their way in almost total darkness. They have developed powerful senses to help them to survive in the dark. Some snakes, for example, locate food by using heat sensors that help them detect small animals, like rats and birds, that are warmer than the surroundings. Some animals, like alligators and owls, can see better at night.

Other nocturnal animals come out at night to avoid the heat and bright light of the day. This is the best time for them to hunt for food, too, when they're protected under a cloak of darkness.

Tonight, we won't go to bed. We'll stay up all night and visit one of the Florida Keys, which are islands off the coast of Florida. Come with us for a closer look at the sights and sounds of the beach in late springtime. We'll witness the amazing things that happen on the beach at nighttime.

We arrive at the beach at dusk when the twilight sky is splashed with sherbet-colored shades of red, pink, and blue. The fiery sun is beginning to slip beneath the horizon.

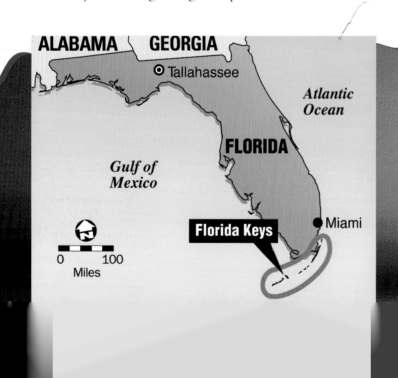

Earlier, the beach was crowded with people. Now the birds have taken over! Caw, caw, caw, the seagulls cry. The sanderlings, like tiny clockwork toys, chase the waves back and forth. Nearby, a skinny-legged, long-beaked willet bird pecks in the sand, looking for fiddler crabs and worms.

Dunes

Marshland

6

Maritime Forest

Mangrove

A Home for Everyone

There's more to an ocean beach environment than sand and water. You may see windswept dunes, marshes, and freshwater rivers. Surrounding the beach there may be mangroves and maritime forests.

Not all animals share the same environment. Some animals, like whales, sharks, and barracudas, live deep beneath the ocean's surface. Others, like hermit crabs and shorebirds, make sandy beaches their home. Worms, barnacles, and tiny shrimp can be found in mudflats and tide pools. Other animals live in the dunes, marshes, freshwater rivers, woods, and lagoons surrounding the beach.

Each habitat is important to different animals. This is because each animal has different requirements for food, water, and shelter.

We watch as a pelican glides high above the waves, looking for dinner. Suddenly, he plunges head first into the water. Splash! The pelican uses his pouch like a net, scooping up fish. When the pelican surfaces, his pouch has expanded like a balloon, filled with seawater. We notice a tiny silver fish wiggling in the pelican's bill. Sometimes, seagulls snatch a pelican's catch before he has a chance to swallow it, but not this time! The pelican quickly snaps his head back and gobbles the fish.

Pelicans: High-Flying Divers

Brown pelicans are famous for their plunging dives. They can dive from as high as 60 feet above the water. Pelicans have huge, expandable pouches that can hold up to three gallons of water. Brown pelicans are never far from the water, where they feed on small fish.

At one time, brown pelicans were endangered in the United States. The major cause was pesticide poisoning. Brown pelicans are common on the East Coast but are still listed as endangered in some parts of North America. Today, the main threats to pelicans are being caught in fishing lines and flying into overhead wires.

It's low tide and the dark and gooey mudflats near the lagoon are teeming with life. A brown and white striped periwinkle snail clings to a rock. Did you know that snails release a slimy covering over their bodies when the tide goes out? This prevents them from drying up.

High tide

Low tide

What Causes the Tides?

Tides in the ocean are caused by the pull of the moon and the sun on Earth. The moon and the sun pull ocean water toward them.

High tide occurs when ocean water reaches its highest point on the coast. High tide usually occurs when the moon is directly over the earth. Low tide occurs when ocean water reaches its lowest point on the coast. Tides are usually lowest during a new or full moon.

High and low tide happen two times a day (about every 12 hours). These times change each day, but people can predict when the high and low tides will occur each day.

The longer we look in the tidal pool, the more we see. The mudflats are full of oysters and clams. Oysters and clams are mollusks. Mollusks have soft bodies protected by hard outer shells. Snails are mollusks, too.

There is a colony of barnacles stuck to an empty shell. These barnacles will live on this same shell for their entire lives. They will not move. Instead, they wait for the tide to wash in plankton for them to eat.

Hundreds of worms and tiny amphipods wiggle and squirm in the mud. Amphipods look like insects, and most have seven pairs of legs. Some amphipods have legs on their tails to help them jump.

13

Several creatures lurk in the shadows of the sand dunes.
Gopher tortoises are crawling into underground burrows to
hide from predators and to protect themselves from the weather.
Nearby, an endangered Eastern indigo snake slithers out of the
mangrove swamp. Its glossy, blue-black skin has scales that
shine in the moonlight. The Eastern indigo snake is the largest
snake in North America. It can grow to be eight feet long.
During the winter, Eastern indigo snakes live in abandoned
gopher tortoise burrows.

14

Eastern indigo snake

Gopher Tortoises: Wildlife Landlords

The gopher tortoise is a cold-blooded reptile that feeds mostly on grasses, flowers, and fruits. It averages about 10 inches long and weighs about 9 pounds. The shell of the tortoise is part of its skeleton. It uses its shell as a hiding spot from predators when it can't make it back to its burrow.

Tortoises can live to be 40 to 60 years old. They are a threatened species, except in Florida, where they are more plentiful. Tortoises need large areas of land, with plenty of food and room to dig burrows.

One of the reasons tortoises are important is that they spread the seeds of many plants. Also, they are called "wildlife landlords," because their burrows are used by other animals as resting or hiding spots.

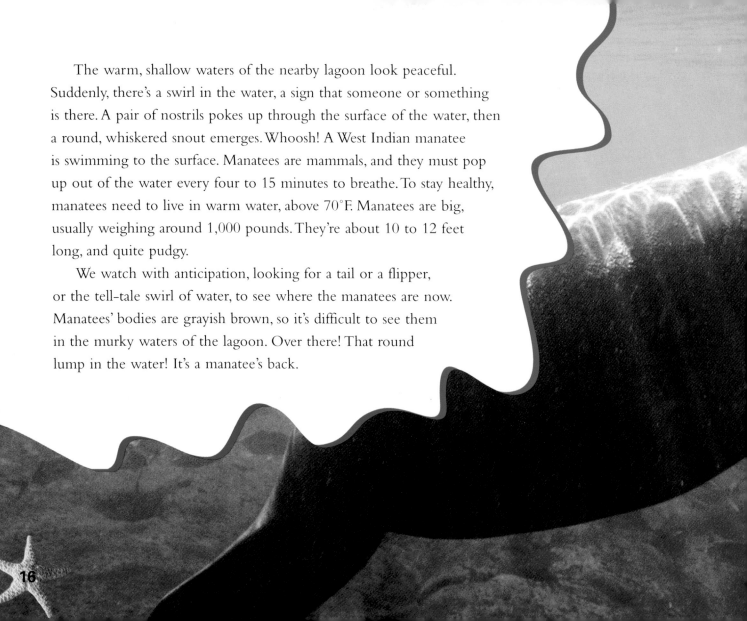

The warm, shallow waters of the nearby lagoon look peaceful.
Suddenly, there's a swirl in the water, a sign that someone or something
is there. A pair of nostrils pokes up through the surface of the water, then
a round, whiskered snout emerges. Whoosh! A West Indian manatee
is swimming to the surface. Manatees are mammals, and they must pop
up out of the water every four to 15 minutes to breathe. To stay healthy,
manatees need to live in warm water, above 70°F. Manatees are big,
usually weighing around 1,000 pounds. They're about 10 to 12 feet
long, and quite pudgy.

We watch with anticipation, looking for a tail or a flipper,
or the tell-tale swirl of water, to see where the manatees are now.
Manatees' bodies are grayish brown, so it's difficult to see them
in the murky waters of the lagoon. Over there! That round
lump in the water! It's a manatee's back.

Disappearing Manatees

Manatees are gentle giants, with no natural enemies. Sadly, the manatees are disappearing. They are on the list of endangered species. Long ago, manatees were hunted for their flesh, bones, and hide. Now, boats are the manatee's biggest threat. Speeding boats run over many manatees that are submerged under the water, killing them by impact or cutting into their backs with the propellers. Nearly all of the manatees in the wild have scars on their bodies caused by accidents with boats.

Natural events also endanger manatees. When winters are unusually cold, manatees die because their bodies cannot survive long in cold water. When the water temperature drops below 60°F, manatees stop eating. But usually manatees are able to move to warmer waters in the South. Many people are working to help save the manatees, so they will not become extinct.

Just a short distance offshore, we see a pod of frolicking dolphins. One dolphin jumps completely out of the water, as he chases a flying mullet fish. Another dolphin playfully flips her baby into the air. Dolphins are social animals. They love to play and interact with each other. If we could see under the water, we might see the dolphins playing follow-the-leader, or doing barrel-rolls.

Bottlenose Dolphins: Water Acrobats

Watching a pod of dolphins arching their sleek bodies and jumping out of the water is a special sight. Bottlenose dolphins can jump up to 20 feet in the air and dive down more than 1,000 feet into the water.

Bottlenose dolphins grow to about 9 feet and weigh about 400 pounds. They breathe through a single blowhole near the top of their head. Each dolphin has a unique whistle, which never changes and is used to identify it for its entire life.

Dolphins send out various sounds and use the returning echoes to locate their prey. The dolphin can pick up sound through every inch of its skin. Dolphins also have an excellent sense of smell.

Today, bottlenose dolphins are abundant in coastal waters and can live to be about 25 years old.

What a strange sight this is! Fierce-looking creatures with spiked tails are crawling out of the lagoon. The dark, hard-shell animals look like horses' hooves. They patrol the shallow waters, using their long tails to plow through the wet sand. These horseshoe crabs are looking for worms and mollusks. Horseshoe crabs feed mostly at night.

One of the horseshoe crabs has flipped itself over and we see his soft underbelly, a dozen legs, and a large flap. This flap hides nearly 200 gills. The horseshoe crab gets oxygen from the water and air by using these gills.

The horseshoe crab does not stay belly-up for long. He quickly thrusts his tail into the sand and flips back over.

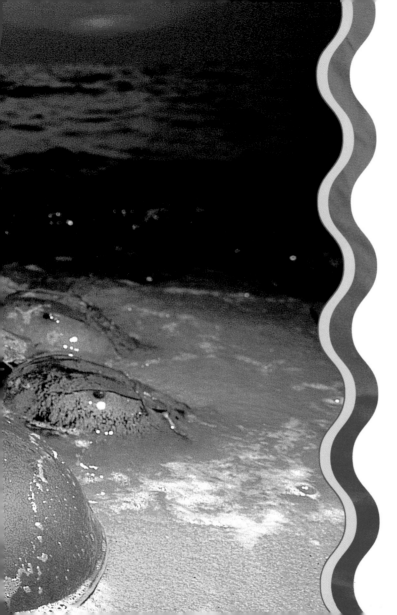

Horseshoe Crabs: Living Fossils

Horseshoe crabs have been around for more than 300 million years, even longer than the dinosaurs. One of the reasons they have survived for so many years is because of their hard shells. Like many animals with shells, a horseshoe crab outgrows its shell and grows a new one. This is called molting. When it is time to molt, the old shell splits around the front edge and the crab crawls out. After 16 molts, the horseshoe crab is fully grown.

The horseshoe crab's long tail is called a telson. Some people think the tail is poisonous or has a stinger, but this is not true. Horseshoe crabs are gentle, harmless animals. Horseshoe crabs are eaten by loggerhead turtles, and their eggs are an important source of food for migrating shorebirds.

Night is fallen. Inky sky meets deep purple ocean. Moonbeams cast silvery shimmers of light on rhythmic waves. Surf tickles shore, surging ever closer to seagrass-fringed dunes as the evening tide comes in.

Now you see it! Now you don't! It's a ghost crab—the beach phantom. It's called a ghost crab because it can vanish right before your eyes. The ghost crab moves quickly, at speeds of 10 miles per hour. Ghost crabs can "hide" right out in the open. Their sandy-beige color blends in with the beach, offering camouflage from preying birds.

Out pops the ghost crab again, its two large black eyes sticking up like periscopes. The ghost crab can look in many directions at once. It can see so well, it can—gulp!—snatch an insect in midair.

Ghost crab

22

In the distance, we hear a deep, rumbling sound. Is it thunder? No. It's the call of several male alligators, letting the female alligators know they are ready to mate.

If we got closer (we won't), we'd smell an unusual odor around the alligators. This smell, though odd to us, is attractive to female alligators.

24

Alligators: 140 Million Years and Counting

Alligators

The American alligators living in Florida today are related to ancient creatures that lived among the dinosaurs. Scientists have discovered skulls belonging to these extinct reptiles that are more than six feet long! Alligators look like large lizards, with black or gray scaly skin. An alligator has a large mouth and a strong jaw, with 70 to 80 long, pointed teeth. They don't chew or grind their food, though. They usually swallow it whole. Alligators eat all kinds of fish, birds, and mammals.

Alligators like to bask in the sun. Their habitat is freshwater rivers, lakes, canals, ponds, and swamps. If a human approaches, an alligator will probably make a quick jump into the water. An alligator's thrashing tail can break a human's leg, and its powerful jaws can easily crush a limb.

Under the cover of darkness, a female loggerhead sea turtle heaves her heavy body out of the surf and onto the shore. Slowly, she pushes her body over the sand with her flippers, crawling past the high tide line, looking for a safe place to lay her eggs. She herself may have been hatched on this very same stretch of beach. Scientists believe that sea turtles remember the smell of the sand where they hatched, and return to that place when it's their turn to bear young.

Three Species of Sea Turtles

Sea turtles are among the oldest living reptiles. Some sea turtle fossils are more than 150 million years old.

Seven species of sea turtles live in the world. Three species of sea turtles make their nests on the coast of Florida—the leatherback, the loggerhead, and the green sea turtle.

Leatherbacks are the largest of all sea turtles. They are also the heaviest reptiles in the world. Leatherbacks can be more than eight feet long and can weigh more than 1,000 pounds. Leatherbacks travel greater distances than any other sea turtle. They also make the deepest dives. Leatherbacks can dive as deep as 3,000 feet.

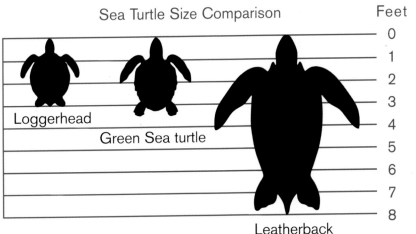

Sea Turtle Size Comparison

Feet: 0, 1, 2, 3, 4, 5, 6, 7, 8

Loggerhead

Green Sea turtle

Leatherback

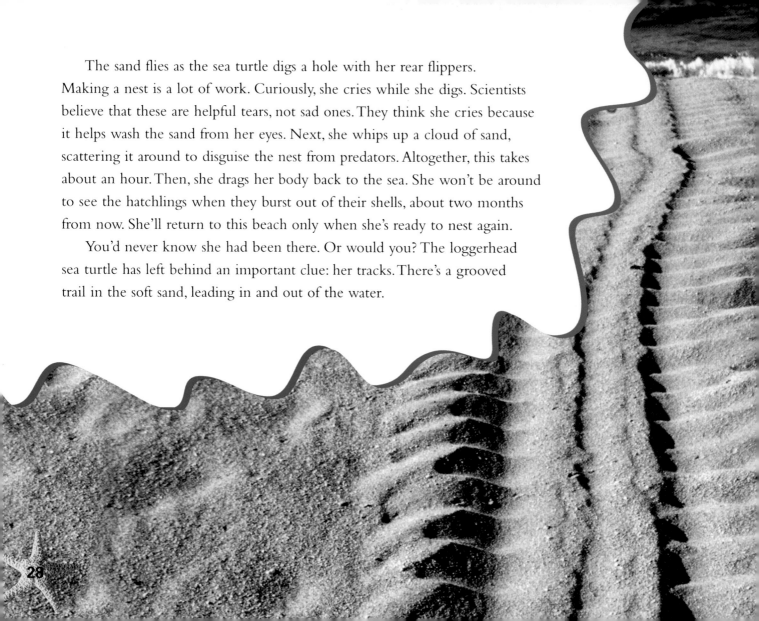

The sand flies as the sea turtle digs a hole with her rear flippers. Making a nest is a lot of work. Curiously, she cries while she digs. Scientists believe that these are helpful tears, not sad ones. They think she cries because it helps wash the sand from her eyes. Next, she whips up a cloud of sand, scattering it around to disguise the nest from predators. Altogether, this takes about an hour. Then, she drags her body back to the sea. She won't be around to see the hatchlings when they burst out of their shells, about two months from now. She'll return to this beach only when she's ready to nest again.

You'd never know she had been there. Or would you? The loggerhead sea turtle has left behind an important clue: her tracks. There's a grooved trail in the soft sand, leading in and out of the water.

Loggerheads and Green Sea Turtles

Loggerheads are the most common sea turtles. Loggerhead sea turtles are about three feet long, and usually weigh 150 to 350 pounds. They are called loggerheads because they have large heads compared to other sea turtles. Their heads may be 10 inches wide. Loggerheads have very powerful jaws to crush food, such as horseshoe crabs.

Green sea turtles have different diets than other adult sea turtles. They eat only plants. Green sea turtles are about $3\frac{1}{2}$ feet long and weigh about 300 pounds. They are named for the green color of their body fat.

Loggerhead turtle

Green Sea turtle

A raccoon scampers from his hiding place behind a patch of sea oats. He's been waiting and watching. Time for a snack! With the black mask of a burglar, the fearless raccoon lunges at the turtle's nest, scooping and flinging sand with his paws. Soon, tasty, fresh turtle eggs will be his . . . "Scat! Get out of here!"

The turtle patrol has arrived, shooing away the raccoon before he unearthed his prize. A park ranger and a volunteer are walking the beach, looking for turtle nests. They fit the nests with wire screens to protect them from predators. Tonight, they arrived just in time.

The raccoon moves on, looking for an easier target. There is plenty of food for a raccoon on this island, mainly because raccoons eat almost anything—insects, frogs, crayfish, bird eggs, fruits, nuts, and food that people leave behind in trash barrels.

Tumbling Turtles

What happens to the sea turtle eggs after the mother leaves the nest? In about 60 days, as many as 100 tiny turtles will wiggle out of the nest and tumble into the sand. Hatching is triggered by temperature. Sea turtles usually hatch between 11 P.M. and 2 A.M., when the sand is cool.

Then, guided by the light of the moon, they will march to the warm Atlantic surf. When they reach the water, the hatchlings paddle until they reach the Gulf Stream, swimming with the current. Sea turtles spend most of their lives in the ocean. They grow, eat, and mate in the water.

Loggerhead turtle hatchlings

It's daybreak. Sun rays dance on the surf, bouncing light through the early morning fog. The nocturnal animals have returned to their hiding spots.

The beach is littered with sea wrack. Sea wrack is the seaweed and other things left on the beach after a high tide.

Among the weeds we find shells with clinging barnacles, tiny sea horses, and scurrying crabs. The high tide and strong winds have brought in many specimens of purple-colored Portuguese man-of-war. They look like small inflated balloons scattered on the beach.

Danger: Purple Balloon on the Beach!

If you see something that looks like a purple balloon on the beach, don't pick it up. It's probably a Portuguese man-of-war, a relative of jellyfish that can give you a nasty sting, even when it's dead.

A Portuguese man-of-war has long feeding tentacles designed to sting and stun prey. These tentacles can stretch up to 50 feet. Floating on the ocean, the man-of-war's soft, blue body makes it difficult to see against the water. Usually, they live far out to sea, but strong winds and currents carry them onto the beach, where they are eaten by mole crabs and ghost crabs.

The Portuguese man-of-war got its name because early explorers thought its shape looked like the helmets worn by Portuguese soldiers.

Portuguese man-of-war

What else has the tide brought to shore? The beach is full of treasures from the deep sea. Several mermaid's purses are scattered among the seaweed. Mermaid's purses are cases that once contained the eggs of fish. They got their name because they look like old-fashioned coin purses.

Thousands of pearly, multi-colored coquinas, or bean clams, nestle in the sand, awaiting the next wave. The rich splash of water provides the food and oxygen they need to survive.

Sea beans, fallen from the trees and vines in far-away places, have also washed ashore. Some people believe that sea beans carry good luck.

Mermaid's purses

Coquinas

Cool Beans

Question: When is a bean not a bean?
Answer: When it's a sea bean. Also known as drift seeds, sea beans are the seeds of trees and vines that grow along tropical coastlines around the world. The seeds fall from plants into major rivers and streams, eventually drifting into the ocean. Sea beans travel for miles and miles, floating with ocean currents, and finally wash up on a faraway beach.

Sea beans come in all shapes and sizes. Some rattle when you shake them, some don't. Since they are hard, they can withstand long, wet journeys.

Sea beans are most bountiful after higher-than-normal tides during the hurricane season. Look for sea beans after the tide goes out. If you pick through the seaweed, driftwood, and other stuff, you might be rewarded with a handful of mystery seeds.

A large black and white bird soars high in the sky, its wings stretching nearly five feet across. Its beady yellow eyes are focused on the water below. It's an osprey hunting for an early morning meal. There's something appetizing . . . a tiny fish swimming in the shallows. The osprey stalls in the air, then flaps its wings before diving feet first into the water. Osprey have barbs on their feet that help them grab and hold slippery fish. The osprey flaps off to its nest, with the fish dangling in its talons.

Then something moving in the shimmering ocean surf catches our eye. It's a manta ray launching its massive black and white body!

Manta Rays: Underwater Gliders

Manta rays glide through the ocean like underwater birds. Their wingspans can reach up to 20 feet. Manta rays are related to sharks, though. They are one of the largest creatures in the ocean.

Manta rays have flat, broad, streamlined bodies. Some people think they look like blankets moving through the water. The name "manta" means "cloak" in Spanish. Their side fins are wide and triangle-shaped, like wings. Mantas were called "devil fish" by sailors who saw large horns extending from the fish's head. These body parts are not really horns, but scoopers, which the manta uses to guide plankton into its mouth.

Manta rays are a favorite sight for divers. Manta rays can sometimes be seen in shallower waters off the beach. They live in warm waters.

Manta ray

The beach may look the same as it did yesterday, but actually it changes every single day. A coastal island is always changing. Some changes are dramatic and happen very quickly. A powerful hurricane can slice a channel into the land where none existed before. Crashing waves can flatten sand dunes. Careless people may trample the grasses that hold the dune in place.

Some changes are more gradual. Over time, wind and waves are natural sculptors, capable of reshaping an island. Here, blowing sand builds up a ripply dune. There, a foamy wave deposits a vibrant scatter of shells. The plants and animals that live on the beach are well-adapted to their ever-changing world.

Perhaps someday we'll return to this spectacular stretch of beach. But it won't be the same. It will be wild and beautiful in a different way.

Index